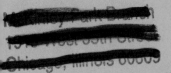

ank.

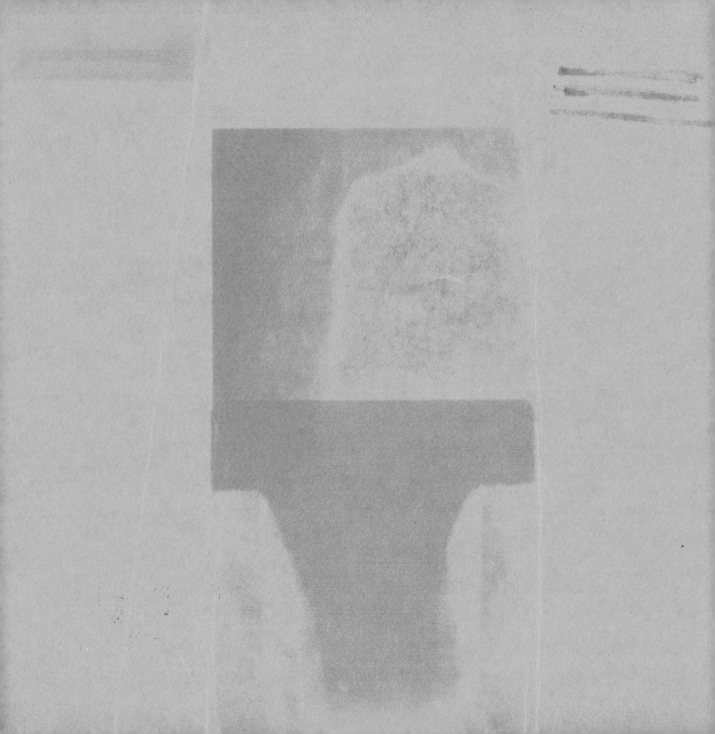

GREEDYANNA

GREEDYANNA

Frank Remkiewicz

Lothrop, Lee & Shepard Books   **New York**

To Grace

Copyright © 1992 by Frank Remkiewicz

Printed in the United States of America.
First Edition 1 2 3 4 5 6 7 8 9 10
Library of Congress Cataloging in Publication Data
Remkiewicz, Frank.   Greedyanna / by Frank Remkiewicz.
p.   cm.   Summary: Anna is going through a phase where she wants everything for herself, except
the lima beans.   ISBN 0-688-10294-8.—ISBN 0-688-10295-6 (lib. bdg.)   (1. Greed—Fiction.
2. Brothers and sisters—Fiction.)
I. Title.   PZ7.R2835Gr   1992   (E)—dc20 91-14923 CIP AC

"Mine! Mine! Mine!" said Anna. She
stacked our pork chops on her plate.

"Anna is going through a phase, Eddie,"
said Dad. "Don't say anything. She'll get
over it."

"Mine! Mine! Mine!" She scooped up all
our noodles.

"Here, have my limas too," said Mom.
"No!" said Anna. Anna doesn't like lima
beans. Neither do I.

It wasn't just our food that Anna wanted.

It was everything! Some phase.

We moved into the garage. "Just for a while," said Dad. "This phase won't last long."

Mom bought a case of lima beans so we'd have plenty of food.

"Her name should be GREEDYANNA!" I said.

Mom said maybe if we went to the
beach, Anna would forget her phase and
we'd all have fun. Oh, sure. Greedyanna
wanted each and every seat in the car.

But we solved that problem.

"Mine!" said Anna in the ocean.

"Mine!" said Anna on the sand.

It was hot pushing the car home, so we stopped for ice cream. Anna let us keep our napkins. I thought maybe that was a good sign. I was wrong.

We went to the park to ride the little train.

Dad had to buy twenty-four tickets.

"How about a camping trip," suggested Dad.
"Maybe she'll meet a nice hungry grizzly
bear," I said. Pushing the car to the state park
was easier when I thought about the bear.

We made a great campfire. Dad said
lima beans tasted better when you cooked
them outdoors.

Anna took the whole tent for herself, so we slept under the car.

We could see the whole night sky and the bottoms of the car door handles. Mom said there must be a million stars.

"Don't tell Greedyanna," I told her.

The garage seemed clean and cozy after three nights under the car. Dad fired up the barbecue while Mom got the shish-ka-bobs started. We could hear Greedyanna stomping around the house.

Then the door flew open and she
stormed in. A tear rolled down her cheek,
all the way to her lip. She ate it.

"I'm lonesome!" Greedyanna wailed.
"Can I stay here with you?"

Mom hugged Anna
and Dad picked her up.
She stopped crying.

"Have some barbecued limas," I said.
"Yum," said Anna.

After supper we all moved back to the house.

Anna gave us presents. "For you," she said. "Yours, yours, and...

THE END
(of a phase)